Stephanie Catwell

The Yawning Traveller

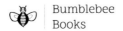
Bumblebee
Books

BUMBLEBEE PAPERBACK EDITION
Copyright © Stephanie Catwell 2023
Illustrations by Megvin Gjovari

A CIP catalogue record for this title is
available from the British Library.

ISBN: 978-1-83934-899-0

Bumblebee Books is an imprint of
Olympia Publishers.

First Published in 2023

Bumblebee Books
Tallis House
2 Tallis Street
London
EC4Y 0AB

Printed in Great Britain

Dedication

For Kyla, my own curious adventurer.

The girl who couldn't sleep
Quickly came to find,
That her yawns created portals
To lands throughout time.

On Monday her yawn
Took her to the first Olympic Games,
Where she won gold in the sprints
And became a household name.

On Tuesday her yawn
Let her walk among the dinosaurs.
She let out mighty roars, sharpened her claws
And befriended herbivores.

On Wednesday her yawn
Transported her to Rome,
Where gladiators battled
In a colosseum they called home.

On Thursday her yawn
Took her to Glastonbury 1993,
Where she danced to Velvet Underground
And camped in a tepee.

On Friday her yawn
Led her to Hercules side,
Where tales of Zeus and Hera
Kept her entertained while the Hydra died.

On Saturday her yawn
Shot her to the moon.
She frolicked in the sea of tranquillity
And floated like a balloon.

On Sunday her yawn
Propelled her forwards in time,
Where she saw glimpses of her life
And finally slept, knowing she'd be fine.

About the Author

Stephanie Catwell is a writer and mother, working to find the magic in everyday moments. She lives in London.